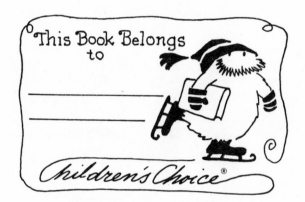

This Book Belongs
to

_____

_____

Children's Choice ®

Sylvester
and the
Magic Pebble

by WILLIAM STEIG

Windmill Books/Simon and Schuster

New York

To Maggie, Lucy, and Jemmy

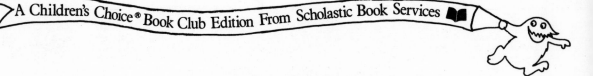

Published by Windmill Books / Simon and Schuster
Rockefeller Center, 630 Fifth Avenue
New York, New York 10020
ISBN: 0-590-75740-7

Sylvester Duncan lived with his mother and father at Acorn Road in Oatsdale. One of his hobbies was collecting pebbles of unusual shape and color.

On a rainy Saturday during vacation he found a quite extraordinary one. It was flaming red, shiny, and perfectly round, like a marble. As he was studying this remarkable pebble, he began to shiver, probably from excitement, and the rain felt cold on his back. "I wish it would stop raining," he said.

To his great surprise the rain stopped. It didn't stop gradually as rains usually do. It CEASED. The drops vanished on the way down, the clouds disappeared, everything was dry, and the sun was shining as if rain had never existed.

In all his young life Sylvester had never had a wish gratified so quickly. It struck him that magic must be at work, and he guessed that the magic must be in the remarkable-looking red pebble. (Where indeed it was.) To make a test, he put the pebble on the ground and said, "I wish it would rain again." Nothing happened. But when he said the same thing holding the pebble in his hoof, the sky turned black, there was lightning and a clap of thunder, and the rain came shooting down.

"What a lucky day this is!" thought Sylvester. "From now on I can have anything I want. My father and mother can have anything they want. My relatives, my friends, and anybody at all can have everything anybody wants!"

He wished the sunshine back in the sky, and he wished a wart on his left hind fetlock would disappear, and it did, and he started home, eager to amaze his father and mother with his magic pebble. He could hardly wait to see their faces. Maybe they wouldn't even believe him at first.

As he was crossing Strawberry Hill, thinking of some of the many, many things he could wish for, he was startled to see a mean, hungry lion looking right at him from behind some tall grass. He was frightened. If he hadn't been so frightened, he could have made the lion disappear, or he could have wished himself safe at home with his father and mother.

He could have wished the lion would turn into a butter-
fly or a daisy or a gnat. He could have wished many things,
but he panicked and couldn't think carefully.

"I wish I were a rock," he said, and he became a rock.

The lion came bounding over, sniffed the rock a hun-
dred times, walked around and around it, and went away
confused, perplexed, puzzled, and bewildered. "I saw that
little donkey as clear as day. Maybe I'm going crazy," he
muttered.

And there was Sylvester, a rock on Strawberry Hill, with the magic pebble lying right beside him on the ground, and he was unable to pick it up. "Oh, how I wish I were myself again," he thought, but nothing happened. He had to be touching the pebble to make the magic work, but there was nothing he could do about it.

His thoughts began to race like mad. He was scared and worried. Being helpless, he felt hopeless. He imagined all the possibilities, and eventually he realized that his only chance of becoming himself again was for someone to find the red pebble and to wish that the rock next to it would be a donkey. Someone would surely find the red pebble — it was so bright and shiny — but what on earth would make them wish that a rock were a donkey? The chance was one in a billion at best.

Sylvester fell asleep. What else could he do? Night came with many stars.

Meanwhile, back at home, Mr. and Mrs. Duncan paced the floor, frantic with worry. Sylvester had never come home later than dinner time. Where could he be? They stayed up all night wondering what had happened, expecting that Sylvester would surely turn up by morning. But he didn't, of course. Mrs. Duncan cried a lot and Mr. Duncan did his best to soothe her. Both longed to have their dear son with them.

"I will never scold Sylvester again as long as I live," said Mrs. Duncan, "no matter what he does."

At dawn, they went about inquiring of all the neighbors.

They talked to all the children — the puppies, the kittens, the colts, the piglets. No one had seen Sylvester since the day before yesterday.

They went to the police. The police could not find their child.

All the dogs in Oatsdale went searching for him. They
sniffed behind every rock and tree and blade of grass, into
every nook and gully of the neighborhood and beyond, but

found not a scent of him. They sniffed the rock on Strawberry Hill, but it smelled like a rock. It didn't smell like
Sylvester.

After a month of searching the same places over and over again, and inquiring of the same animals over and over again, Mr. and Mrs. Duncan no longer knew what to do. They concluded that something dreadful must have happened and that they would probably never see their son again. (Though all the time he was less than a mile away.)

They tried their best to be happy, to go about their
usual ways. But their usual ways included Sylvester and they
were always reminded of him. They were miserable. Life
had no meaning for them any more.

Night followed day and day followed night over and
over again. Sylvester on the hill woke up less and less often.
When he was awake, he was only hopeless and unhappy.

He felt he would be a rock forever and he tried to get used
to it. He went into an endless sleep. The days grew colder.
Fall came with the leaves changing color. Then the leaves
fell and the grass bent to the ground.

Then it was winter. The winds blew, this way and that.
It snowed. Mostly, the animals stayed indoors, living on the
food they had stored up.

One day a wolf sat on the rock that was Sylvester and
howled and howled because he was hungry.

Then the snows melted. The earth warmed up in the
spring sun and things budded.

Leaves were on the trees again. Flowers showed their young faces.

One day in May, Mr. Duncan insisted that his wife go with him on a picnic. "Let's cheer up," he said. "Let us try to live again and be happy even though Sylvester, our angel, is no longer with us." They went to Strawberry Hill.

Mrs. Duncan sat down on the rock. The warmth of his own mother sitting on him woke Sylvester up from his deep winter sleep. How he wanted to shout, "Mother! Father! It's me, Sylvester, I'm right here!" But he couldn't talk. He had no voice. He was stone-dumb.

Mr. Duncan walked aimlessly about while Mrs. Duncan
set out the picnic food on the rock — alfalfa sandwiches,
pickled oats, sassafras salad, timothy compote. Suddenly Mr.
Duncan saw the red pebble. "What a fantastic pebble!" he
exclaimed. "Sylvester would have loved it for his collection."
He put the pebble on the rock.

They sat down to eat. Sylvester was now as wide awake as a donkey that was a rock could possibly be. Mrs. Duncan felt some mysterious excitement. "You know, Father," she said suddenly, "I have the strangest feeling that our dear Sylvester is still alive and not far away."

"I am, I am!" Sylvester wanted to shout, but he couldn't. If only he had realized that the pebble resting on his back was the magic pebble!

"Oh, how I wish he were here with us on this lovely May day," said Mrs. Duncan. Mr. Duncan looked sadly at the ground. "Don't you wish it too, Father?" she said. He looked at her as if to say, "How can you ask such a question?"

Mr. and Mrs. Duncan looked at each other with great sorrow.

"I wish I were myself again, I wish I were my real self again!" thought Sylvester.

And in less than an instant, he was!

You can imagine the scene that followed — the embraces, the kisses, the questions, the answers, the loving looks, and the fond exclamations!

When they had eventually calmed down a bit, and had gotten home, Mr. Duncan put the magic pebble in an iron safe. Some day they might want to use it, but really, for now, what more could they wish for? They all had all that they wanted.

The End

Please turn the page.

Look Who's Part of the Children's Choice® Family!

Something special for Children's Choice® Book Club members

You can get all these storybook favorites—Puss in Boots, Babar, Curious George, Lyle, George and Martha and The Year at Maple Hill Farm—to hang up on your wall. They're big (17″ × 22″) and beautiful posters, printed in full color on high quality paper. Best of all, you can get all 6 for just $3.95, including postage and handling.

To order your set of 6 Children's Choice® posters, please send your name, address and $3.95 in check or money order to:

CHILDREN'S CHOICE® POSTERS
2931 East McCarty St.
P.O. Box 1068
Jefferson City, Mo. 65102

Please allow 3-6 weeks for delivery. Your posters are mailed in a tube, so they won't be creased at all.

Offer expires June 1, 1980